To Peter Orton, with love and appreciation   KH and HC

PUFFIN BOOKS

Published by the Penguin Group
Penguin Books Ltd, 80 Strand, London WC2R 0RL, England
Penguin Putnam Inc., 375 Hudson Street, New York, New York 10014, USA
Penguin Books Australia Ltd, 250 Camberwell Road, Camberwell, Victoria 3124, Australia
Penguin Books Canada Ltd, 10 Alcorn Avenue, Toronto, Ontario, Canada M4V 3B2
Penguin Books India (P) Ltd, 11 Community Centre, Panchsheel Park, New Delhi – 110 017, India
Penguin Books (NZ) Ltd, Cnr Rosedale and Airborne Roads, Albany, Auckland, New Zealand
Penguin Books (South Africa) (Pty) Ltd, 24 Sturdee Avenue, Rosebank 2196, South Africa

Penguin Books Ltd, Registered Offices: 80 Strand, London WC2R 0RL, England

www.penguin.com

First published in hardback 2002
Published in paperback 2003
5 7 9 10 8 6 4

Made and printed in Italy by Printer Trento Srl

British Library Cataloguing in Publication Data
A CIP catalogue record for this book is available from the British Library

ISBN 0–140–56912–X

To find out more about Angelina, visit her web site at **www.angelinaballerina.com**

Angelina and Henry

Story by **Katharine Holabird** Illustrations by **Helen Craig**

PUFFIN BOOKS

Angelina could hardly wait to go camping
in the Big Cat Mountains with Uncle Louie.
"I'll dance under the stars," she smiled as
she spun around the room.

Little cousin Henry showed off his panama hat.
"I'm going to be a great explorer," he announced.

"Are you fit and fearless?" Uncle Louie asked
with a wink. "Big Cat could still be up there."

They set off early the next morning,
with Mrs Mouseling's cheese crumpets
still warm in their pockets.

At first, Angelina skipped and twirled along
the winding trail. Then she noticed Uncle
Louie disappearing up the mountain and
had to race to catch up.

As they climbed higher and higher,
Angelina began to feel very hot
and tired.

Henry happily jogged ahead of her.
"You're too slow, Angelina!"
he teased. "Big Cat will get you."

"My backpack is so heavy,"
moaned Angelina.

"Only another mile or two to go,"
Uncle Louie encouraged her.

At last they reached the top of the mountain, and Angelina collapsed with a sigh.

"We've got to set up camp before sunset," said Uncle Louie, showing Angelina and Henry how to unpack.

"Can we have our campfire now?" Angelina asked hopefully.

"You'll need to collect some wood," Uncle Louie replied, "while I put up the tents."

Henry scampered off into the trees. "Let's explore!" he shouted, waving a stick.

"We have to get the firewood first," Angelina reminded him.

But it was much more fun exploring and soon the two little mouselings were deep in the forest.

They played hide-and-seek and sword-fighting, and then they discovered a secret fort. Before long they'd forgotten all about Uncle Louie and collecting firewood.

When they finally stopped to look around, the forest was growing dark and shadowy. The wind was beginning to whistle and strange shapes loomed behind the trees.

Henry dropped his stick. "I'm hungry," he whimpered.

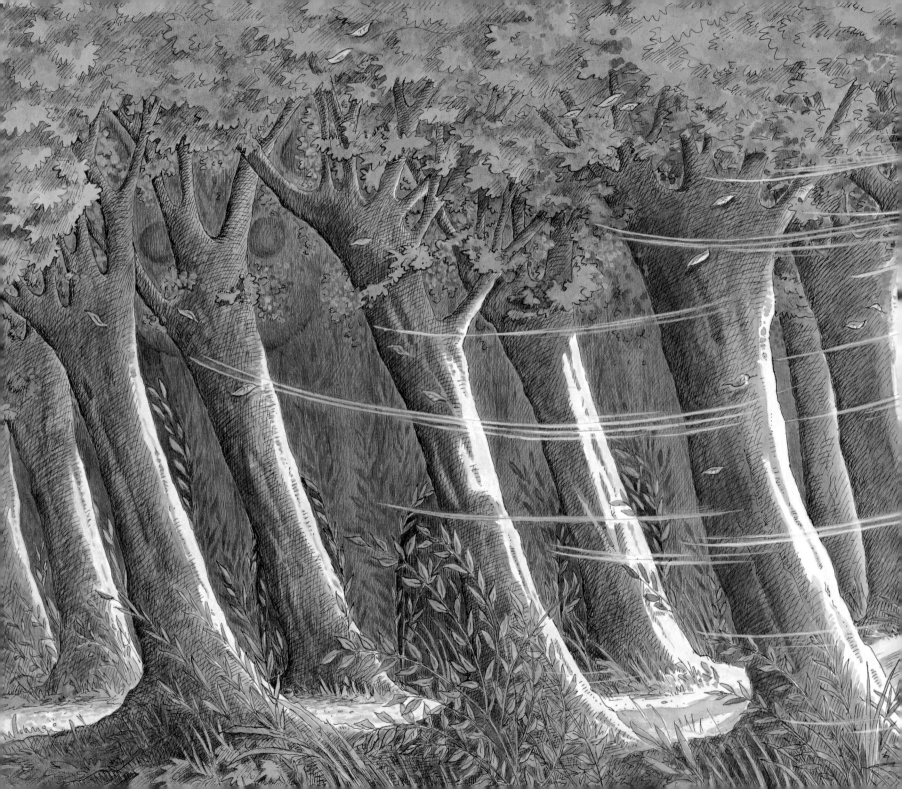

"*Meeeeow*." Something howled behind them.

"What's that?" Henry squeaked. He grabbed Angelina's tail.

Two large ears twitched behind a tree.

"It's just a shadow," whispered Angelina, pulling Henry into the fort.

A black tail flashed by in the wind.

"Big Cat's coming!" wailed Henry, hiding his eyes.

"We'll just have to be brave," said Angelina, and she leapt out into the dark night. "Shoo! Shooo! Shoooooo!" she shouted, waving her sword.

Rain pelted down and thunder roared. Then lightning struck and a big branch crashed to the ground.

Big Cat vanished.

Poor Henry's whiskers were trembling. Angelina held him close and, while the storm raged around them, she made up songs and silly jokes to comfort him.

Finally the wild winds passed. Angelina was soaking wet, but she'd kept Henry cosy and warm. She gathered him up and set off through the woods, calling for Uncle Louie.

Suddenly Angelina stopped. Two yellow eyes were glinting through the trees …

"Angelina! Henry! Thank goodness you're safe."

It was Uncle Louie with two lanterns. He hugged the little mouselings, and then carried Henry to the campsite with Angelina lighting the way.

They all made the bonfire together and had a great feast of chestnuts and Cheddarburgers. Angelina and Henry promised Uncle Louie they'd never run off again, and they told him all about their scary adventure.

After supper, Uncle Louie played tunes on his concertina, while Angelina and Henry danced around the campfire.

Before bedtime, they sat out under the stars.

"I lost my panama hat," Henry said sadly.
"But we really scared off old Big Cat, didn't we?"

"Yes," Angelina agreed. "And that's because we're
both fit and fearless explorers."